DISNEY

CLUB PENGUIN™

Dancing with Cadence

PICK YOUR PATH 5

Disney CLUB PENGUIN™

Dancing with Cadence

PICK YOUR PATH 5

by Tracey West

Grosset & Dunlap

An Imprint of Penguin Group (USA) Inc.

GROSSET & DUNLAP
Published by the Penguin Group
Penguin Group (USA) Inc., 375 Hudson Street, New York,
New York 10014, USA
Penguin Group (Canada), 90 Eglinton Avenue East, Suite 700,
Toronto, Ontario M4P 2Y3, Canada
(a division of Pearson Penguin Canada Inc.)
Penguin Books Ltd., 80 Strand, London WC2R 0RL, England
Penguin Group Ireland, 25 St. Stephen's Green, Dublin 2, Ireland
(a division of Penguin Books Ltd.)
Penguin Group (Australia), 250 Camberwell Road, Camberwell,
Victoria 3124, Australia
(a division of Pearson Australia Group Pty. Ltd.)
Penguin Books India Pvt. Ltd., 11 Community Centre, Panchsheel Park,
New Delhi—110 017, India
Penguin Group (NZ), 67 Apollo Drive, Rosedale,
North Shore 0632, New Zealand
(a division of Pearson New Zealand Ltd.)
Penguin Books (South Africa) (Pty.) Ltd., 24 Sturdee Avenue,
Rosebank, Johannesburg 2196, South Africa

Penguin Books Ltd., Registered Offices:
80 Strand, London WC2R 0RL, England

© 2011 Disney. All rights reserved. Used under license by
Penguin Young Readers Group. Published by Grosset & Dunlap, a division of
Penguin Young Readers Group, 345 Hudson Street, New York, New York 10014.
GROSSET & DUNLAP is a trademark of Penguin Group (USA) Inc.
Printed in the U.S.A.

ISBN 978-0-448-45537-2   10 9 8 7 6 5 4 3 2 1

0 1021 0255826 3

"Two slices of pizza please, extra anchovies," your friend Raj tells the waiter.

You and Raj have come to your favorite hangout spot, the Pizza Parlor. A purple penguin is playing a jazzy tune on the piano. The smell of melted cheese wafts through the air. Every table is filled with penguins talking and eating delicious pizza.

It's Thursday, and you're reading the brand-new edition of *The Club Penguin Times*. As usual, it's packed with information.

"So what's new and exciting?" Raj asks you.

"Lots," you reply. "Check this out. There's a rumor that the Penguin Band is going to be performing a concert at a secret location."

"Let me see that!" Raj cries, scooting closer to you. "I've heard of the Penguin Band, but I've never seen them live before. I wonder how we can find out the secret location."

"The article says there might be clues," you tell him. "But it doesn't say where or when they'll appear."

"Well, we'll have to keep our eyes open," Raj says. "I don't want to miss out on that concert!"

Your waiter arrives with your pizza. Both

slices are piled with anchovies, just how you like it. You put the paper down and take a bite of the piping hot treat.

"Mmm, fishalicious!" you say.

"Totally," Raj agrees between bites. "So, what else is in the news this week?"

"I saved the best for last," you say. "Hold on."

You gulp down the rest of your pizza in one bite. Then you wipe your greasy flippers on a napkin and pick up the paper again.

"It's about Cadence," you say. "She's looking for a dance crew!"

You read the article aloud.

Cadence Announces Rooftop Concert!

Normally, you can find Cadence inside the Night Club, leading the Dance Contest. But this Friday, Cadence will bring her amazing moves to the Night Club roof for a special concert!

"Sometimes you've got to mix things up," Cadence says. "This spectacular show will be a Club Penguin first. But I can't do it by myself. I'm looking for a dance crew to rip up the dance floor with me!"

Cadence will be holding auditions in the

Night Club beginning at 3:00 CPT on Thursday. Do you have what it takes to join Cadence's crew? Then put on your dancing shoes and head to the Night Club!

"Awesome!" Raj says, standing up. "We've got to enter the contest. You and I are great dancers!"

You have to agree. You and Raj practice dance routines almost every day.

"We always get great scores when we enter the Dance Contest," you say. "I know we'd make a great dance crew for Cadence."

Raj looks at his watch. "Oh no!" he cries. "It's already two o'clock (Club Penguin Time). We've only got an hour before the auditions."

"We should head to the Night Club and check out the other crews," you suggest. "We want to make sure the routine we do is fresh."

"Our moves are *already* fresh!" Raj says. "Let's not worry about those other crews. I say we go to the Gift Shop and buy some kickin' new outfits. We need to wow Cadence with our style as well as our moves."

"I wish we had time to do both," you say.

"We could split up," Raj suggests. "You go to the Night Club, and I'll get the outfits for us."

You consider this. It's a good solution, except for one thing. You and Raj have very different styles. You're more sporty, while Raj tends to put together outrageous costumes. If Raj goes to the Gift Shop alone, you're not sure what he'll come back with.

If you go with Raj to the Gift Shop, go to page 28.

If you and Raj split up and meet back at the Night Club, go to page 40.

CONTINUED FROM PAGE 43.

"Let's keep going," you suggest. "Maybe we'll find some signs of the green puffle in the Mine Shack."

You walk inside the Mine Shack, and, to your surprise, you see a green puffle! It's on top of one of the tall posts at the entrance to the Mine, and it looks nervous.

"There you are!" Cadence says. She runs up to the post. But the green puffle doesn't seem to recognize her.

"How did you get all the way up there?" she asks in a soothing voice.

"If it jumps down, we can catch it," you say.

The green puffle looks scared.

"I've got an idea," Cadence says. She turns to you. "Can you give me a beat?"

"Sure," you say. You make your best beat-box sound with your beak, tapping your foot on the floor of the Mine.

Cadence starts to bop up and down with the groove. "Dance with me, puffle. Move to the beat!"

The green puffle relaxes. It starts to hop

up and down to the music.

"Keep that groove movin'!" Cadence says.

You speed up the beat. The green puffle hops higher and higher. Then it hops right off the post!

"Gotcha!" Cadence says, expertly catching the puffle in her arms.

The green puffle smiles at her. Cadence suddenly looks confused.

"Hey, you're not the puffle from the Night Club," she realizes.

Just then, a blue penguin rushes in.

"Oh, Apple, there you are!" she cries. She takes the puffle from Cadence's flippers and hugs it. "Thank you so much for finding her!"

"No prob," Cadence says. "Glad to help."

"You didn't happen to see any other green puffles wandering around, did you?" you ask.

The blue penguin shakes her head. "Nope."

You turn to Cadence. "This was a dead end. Let's go to the Plaza."

Go to page 54.

CONTINUED FROM PAGE 66.

You frown. "We could lose time on this path. Let's keep going to the Ice Rink. Maybe that's where the white puffle was leading us."

Cadence and Raj follow you to the Ice Rink. There's no sign of the white puffle or the green puffle. In fact, the only penguin there is is a lone red penguin on the ice wearing a scarf. She looks sad.

"Have you seen the green puffle from the Night Club here?" you ask.

The penguin shakes her head.

"Hey, you're lookin' like you lost your groove. Everything okay?" Cadence asks.

The red penguin looks up and her face brightens. "Oh wow, Cadence, it's you! I am such a big fan. I love to enter the Dance Contest when I'm at the Night Club."

"Thanks," Cadence says. "So why do you look so down?"

The penguin frowns again. "I'm a terrible skater! I always fall down. I just can't seem to get the hang of it."

"If you can dance, then you can skate,"

Cadence tells her. "It's all about rhythm and balance. If you're good at the Dance Contest, I bet you do the moonwalk, right?"

The red penguin nods.

"Then just imagine you're on the dance floor," Cadence suggests. "Forget there's ice underneath your feet. Just close your eyes, and slide."

Cadence gracefully slides across the ice to demonstrate. The red penguin takes a deep breath and slides on the ice.

"I did it!" she cries happily.

Cadence twirls on the ice. "Try a spin! Just pretend you're on the dance floor."

The red penguin nods and raises her flippers in the air. Then she does a perfect spin.

"That was great!" you say.

"Thanks," the red penguin says shyly. "I didn't think I could do it."

Suddenly, Raj starts jumping up and down. "Look!"

A penguin in a rescue uniform walks into the Ice Rink. He's carrying a yellow puffle in one flipper—and a green puffle in the other! When the green puffle sees Cadence, it joyously jumps into her flippers.

"It's you!" Cadence cries. "Where have you been?"

"These two were caught in an avalanche," the rescue worker explains. "From what I can tell, the yellow puffle was playing its flute and the green puffle was dancing. The vibrations caused a bunch of snow to collapse around them. It was an accident, but nobody got hurt. They were just trapped—until I got there."

"You rock!" Cadence says. "Thanks so much. I'm glad they're both safe."

You're glad, too.

"Does this mean the dance crew auditions are back on?" you ask.

"Yes," Cadence says. "But check this out. I want you two to be in my crew—no auditions necessary!"

Go to page 70.

You'd normally play it safe, but something tells you that Raj is right.

"Okay," you say. "We'll do the Hip-Hop Hurricane."

You help the Smooth Moves guys push the piano aside on the small stage inside the Pizza Parlor. A small crowd gathers to see what's going on. Len sets up a boom box.

"Let's do it as a battle," Raj says boldly. "Your moves against ours."

"You're on!" say Len, Ben, and Ken.

The music starts to play. Len goes first, moonwalking across the stage. Ben does a handstand and then a backflip. Ken sashays across the stage, disco-style, pointing his flipper in the air.

You and Raj look at each other, nod, and step forward. Then you both do a backflip, landing on your backs, then spinning side by side. You move across the stage, still spinning, crisscrossing each other in a figure-eight pattern.

The crowd loves it. Len, Ken, and Ben are amazed.

"Sweet moves," Len tells you. "You two definitely win this."

He hands you the final clue.

Then a pink penguin approaches the stage. It's Cadence!

"That move is fierce," she says. "Can you teach me?"

You can't believe it. Cadence, the best dancer ever, wants a dance lesson from *you*.

"Sure," you say.

You and Raj demonstrate the move to Cadence. Len, Ben, and Ken learn the move, too. Soon you're all spinning on the stage.

You feel really happy. Not only do you get to go to the secret show, but you're dancing with Cadence. It's exactly what you wanted!

THE END

CONTINUED FROM PAGE 47.

"Lean left!" you shout, hoping you're right.

You and Raj lean to the left. The track curves to the right.

Wham! You wipe out, tumbling onto the track. You quickly scramble to get back to your cart. You're steady now, and you make it all the way through the Mine. But when you get to the end, the cart in front of you is empty, and the crab is gone.

"No!" you yell, jumping out of the cart. You check the ground for signs of the crab, but there's nothing.

"There goes our clue," you say with a sigh.

Raj pats you on the back. "Hey, it's cool. We may not get to the concert. But this is an adventure I'll never forget."

You have to smile. Raj is right.

"Come on," you say. "Let's go get some pizza."

THE END

CONTINUED FROM PAGE 57.

"Raj and I are fast learners," you say. "Let's do 'Jet Pack Party' if that's the best one."

Sam and Kat teach you the song. In the background, you hear all kinds of music: rock, funk, hip-hop, and country. Before you know it, it's your turn to go on. The penguin emcee addresses the crowd.

"Give it up for The Migrators!"

Kat counts out the beat on the drums, and the song begins. Sam starts to sing.

"We're going to a jet pack party,
Gonna dance up in the clouds . . ."

You and Raj sing the backup parts.

When you're done, the crowd goes wild. Then the emcee asks the audience to vote for their favorite band by clapping. The Migrators get the most applause of all. You win!

"You really helped us out," Kat tells you and Raj. "You should be in our band permanently."

You and Raj smile at each other. You're in a real band!

THE END

CONTINUED FROM PAGE 69.

"Let's try the Dojo," you suggest. "It's always interesting to watch penguins play *Card-Jitsu*."

"Hmm," Raj says thoughtfully. "Sounds interesting. Let's go!"

The Dojo sits atop a snowy mountain peak. You walk up the large stone steps and past the statues of the meditating puffles. Then you and Raj walk across the courtyard and through the bamboo doors.

Penguins are on the blue practice mats, practicing their best *Card-Jitsu* moves. Before they battle, they press their flippers together and bow out of respect.

You watch some of the practice battles. The competitors use the power of fire, snow, and water to beat one another on the mat.

"Pretty cool," Raj says. "But let's heat things up and enter a *Card-Jitsu Fire* battle."

Since you have both earned your *Card-Jitsu* black belts, you have access to the secret ninja hideout. Once inside, you enter the Fire Room and play *Card-Jitsu Fire* with two other ninjas. It's a harder game, and you see some really advanced moves. There are ninjas poised on one foot, arms raised in attack pose. Other ninjas somersault across the fiery pit to make a perfect landing on a flat stone.

Raj wins the match, and you come in second. But, more importantly, you have the inspiration you need.

"Let's work out a new dance," you say.

You head back to your igloo and play some music on your jukebox. Then you and Raj get to work choreographing your new routine. You pack it with some martial arts moves. You even make up some new moves, like the Water Slide, the Fiery Flip, and the Big Chill. To top it off, you decide to wear your ninja black belts and masks.

Soon it's time for the semifinal round. You head back to the Night Club. It's still crowded with spectators, but now there are only nine other teams competing against you.

Cadence steps onstage.

"Are you penguins ready to move this party?" she asks, and the crowd cheers. "The judges and I will pick the best three crews to make the finals. We'll choose the final crew on Friday, just before the rooftop concert."

Cadence gives each crew a number. You and Raj are number ten, so you'll go last. That means you can watch the competition.

All of the crews are great. One of the crews is made up of three pink penguins that do these great acrobatic moves, flipping and cartwheeling to the music. They're really good. Another talented crew is made up of three penguins in sunglasses and fuzzy wigs. Their footwork is fast and furious.

When it's your turn, you bust out your new martial arts moves. The crowd loves them! The judges love you, too.

"Crew number ten, you're in!" Cadence announces at the end. "See you at the finals."

You and Raj jump up and high-five each other. The other top crews are the pink acrobats and the fuzzy wig guys.

"I think we can beat them," Raj says confidently.

Penguins in the crowd congratulate you. A yellow penguin approaches you.

"You two are the best!" he says. "I've been

watching you through the whole contest. You're amazing!"

"Thanks," you say. "Hey, what's your name?"

"I'm Wiz," he says, a little shyly. "You know, I noticed the other crews have three dancers in them. Maybe I could be your third dancer. I've always dreamed of dancing with Cadence."

"Let's see what you've got," Raj says.

Wiz starts to dance—and he's terrible. He doesn't have any rhythm. He even trips over his own feet!

"What do we do?" you whisper to Raj. "He's so nice. I don't want to hurt his feelings."

Raj shrugs. "I don't know."

If you tell Wiz you're sorry, maybe next time, go to page 38.

If you let Wiz join your crew (and risk losing the contest), go to page 60.

CONTINUED FROM PAGE 55.

"Maybe if we split, the crowd will leave, too," Cadence suggests.

You and Cadence exit the Pizza Parlor. You go all over Club Penguin looking for the green puffle, but no one has seen it.

"I've got an idea," Cadence says. "I'll go talk to Aunt Arctic. I'll see if she can put something in the newspaper about the missing puffle. Catch ya on the flip side!"

A few hours later you see a special edition of *The Club Penguin Times*. It's all about the missing green puffle. A little while later you hear penguins talking.

"Did you hear? They found the puffle!"

Excited, you rush into the Night Club. The green puffle is dancing on top of the speaker. Cadence rushes over to you, smiling.

"Thanks for your help," she says. She hands you a small stuffed puffle. "I got ya something."

"Thanks!" you say. You've always wanted a stuffed puffle!

THE END

CONTINUED FROM PAGE 36.

"Let's try the Coffee Shop first," you say. "If that doesn't work out, we can go to the Pizza Parlor."

The Coffee Shop is crowded with penguins sitting on its red couches, talking and reading the newspaper. You start searching everywhere for clues, but you can't find any. Frustrated, you lean up against the counter.

"How can I help you?" asks a coffee server wearing a green apron.

"You could give us a clue to the location of the Penguin Band's secret concert," you joke.

The server looks serious. "*Sssh!* Not so loud," she says. "I'm the keeper of the Coffee Shop clue. I can give it to you, but first you have to empty the five delivery trucks out back."

You groan. "*Bean Counters*? I'm terrible at that game."

"Your friend can help you," the server says.

You look at Raj. "Let's do it!" he cries.

You play *Bean Counters* with Raj. The first truck rolls in. The bags start flying out pretty quickly. At first, having Raj with you makes things more confusing. You keep bumping into each other.

"Feel the rhythm," Raj tells you. "Like when we do our dance routine."

Raj's advice changes everything. The two of you start to weave around each other smoothly, just like you do on the dance floor. You dodge flying anvils, flowers, and fish. You catch the bags and bring them safely onto the platform.

Soon, all five trucks are empty! You go back to the server, who is happy to give you the next clue.

At this high place you'll find a clue.
It's a special spot with a terrific view.

"The Beacon has a great view," you say.
"So does the top of the Ski Hill," Raj adds.

If you look for the next clue at the Ski Hill, go to page 50.

If you look for the next clue at the Beacon, go to page 58.

CONTINUED FROM PAGE 74.

"I think we can do it with the rope," you say confidently. "You guys stay here while I find one."

You remember that there's plenty of rope lying around at the Lighthouse, so you head there as quickly as you can. You come back with one long, sturdy piece of rope. Then you climb back up the hill.

"Let's all hold on to keep it steady," you tell Cadence and Raj. After everyone grips the rope, you lower it into the hole.

"Chomp down," you tell the puffles. "One at a time."

The yellow puffle goes first. It chomps down on the rope.

"Okay, gently," you tell Cadence and Raj.

You slowly pull on the rope, making sure it doesn't swing from side to side. You pull the yellow puffle through the hole. It lets go of the rope and lands on the hillside. It gives you all a thankful smile.

"Now the green one," you say. You repeat the same procedure, and soon the green puffle is safe, happily jumping into Cadence's lap.

"It's so good to see you!" Cadence says, giving it a hug. "The Night Club just isn't the same without you."

"Looks like the rope was the right way to go," Raj says, giving you a playful punch on the shoulder. "You're pretty smart."

"Aw, it was nothing," you say modestly.

Cadence stands up, still holding the green puffle. "This has been a lot of excitement for one day. I think I'm going to reschedule the dance crew auditions for next week." She looks at you and Raj. "I can't wait to see you guys compete. I bet you can both really tear up the dance floor."

"We won't disappoint you," you promise.

Then Cadence reaches into her scarf and pulls out two envelopes.

"I need to thank you both," she says. "Here are invitations to the secret concert by the Penguin Band."

"No way!" you and Raj cheer.

"The location is still a secret," Cadence tells you. "Even I don't know where it's gonna be. You have to follow clues to find it. The first clue is with your invitation."

You open your envelope and eagerly read what's inside:

If you want to get to the concert on time,
You'll find your next clue in a word in this rhyme.

"I bet the word is *time,*" you guess. "Maybe the next clue is hidden in a clock."

If you look for the next clue in Fred the cuckoo clock, go to page 34.

If you look for the next clue in the Clock Tower, go to page 77.

"You're probably right," you say. "Our routine is already awesome. We don't need to worry about those other crews."

"Great!" Raj says. "Let's head to the Gift Shop."

You tip your waiter and then head out of the Pizza Parlor. As you pass the Stage, which is right next door, Raj suddenly stops and looks at the sign. A revival of *Quest for the Golden Puffle* is playing.

"Cool!" Raj says. "Maybe we can find something in the *Costume Trunk*."

Raj rushes in before you can stop him. Some penguins are practicing, but the play hasn't started yet. Raj opens the *Costume Trunk* and pulls out a mummy costume.

"Awesome!" he cries. Then he pulls the costume over his head. "What do you think? Totally original, right?"

"Definitely original," you agree. "But I'm not sure if a bunch of dancing mummies is what Cadence had in mind."

Raj sees the logic in this. "You're right."

"Come on," you say. "I'm sure we'll find something in the Gift Shop."

It's a short walk to the Town Center. The Gift Shop is filled with penguins trying on the latest fashions from the Penguin Style catalog.

"Check these out!" Raj says, picking two matching Hawaiian shirts from the rack. "These will really help us stand out!"

"Hmm," you say thoughtfully. "They're cool. But we don't want to stand out too much, do we?"

"Of course we do!" Raj says. "We don't want to blend in with the other dance crews."

He goes inside the dressing room and comes out wearing a puffle rainbow–colored snow hat, purple vest, and fluffy boots.

"How about this?" he asks.

"Maybe," you say, but you're not sure.

He tries on another costume. This time he's wearing a hard hat, flip-flops, and a T-shirt with a recycling symbol on it.

"Um, we might have a hard time dancing in flip-flops," you say.

"Good point!" Raj agrees. "All right, then. Do you have any ideas?"

"Let's go to the Winter Sport Shop," you

suggest. "I think a sporty look might be cool."

As you walk to the Winter Sport Shop, you pass by groups of penguins with outrageous outfits. Three penguins are all wearing fairy wings and grass skirts. Another group is wearing bee outfits and bunny slippers.

"I told you," Raj says. "Cool costumes are the key to winning this."

"Let's try my idea," you say.

At the Winter Sport Shop, you pick out blue jerseys and baseball caps, which you put on backward. You finish the outfit with black-and-white sneakers.

"Pretty cool, right?" you ask Raj.

"Sure," Raj says. "But do you think this will help us stand out?"

If you go back and get the mummy costumes, go to page 48.

If you stick with the sporty outfits, go to page 67.

CONTINUED FROM PAGE 55.

"It's up to you," Cadence says.

You look at the poor pizza chef. You are confident you can help her and still find the green puffle.

"Let's make some pizzas," you say. "Come on, I'll show you how."

You lead Cadence inside the kitchen. The order comes up on a screen on the right. The dough comes out of a big machine on the left and rides on a conveyor belt. The sauce, cheese, and toppings are arranged above the belt.

"You take the sauce," you tell Cadence, "and I'll do the cheese and toppings."

"Gotcha," Cadence says confidently.

The pizza chef turns on the machine. "I need forty pizzas!"

The first order pops up: pizza sauce and cheese.

"Just squirt some sauce on it," you tell Cadence.

Cadence obeys, and you add the cheese. A bell rings.

"One down!" you say.

31

"Hey, this isn't so hard," Cadence says.

The orders quickly get more complicated, and the conveyor belt starts moving faster. You stay calm. Five squid? Two seaweed and three shrimp? No problem! You toss them on top of the cheese and get ready for the next order.

Cadence is doing a good job with the sauce, bopping her head in time with the movement of the conveyor belt.

"It's like dancing," she says. "You just have to find your rhythm."

Before you know it, all forty pizzas are done! You step outside the hot kitchen and see happy customers munching on pizza slices.

"Mmm, delicious!"

"Best pizza ever!"

The grateful chef gives you each a hug. "You saved the day! How can I repay you?" she asks.

"You can ask around and see if anyone at the Pizza Parlor has seen the green puffle from the Night Club," you say.

"No problem!" says the chef. She goes from table to table, talking to the customers. Then she brings a red penguin wearing a curly, blond wig to see you.

"Wow, Cadence!" says the blond penguin. "It's so cool to meet you! I hear you're looking for the green puffle. It's a funny thing, but I'm pretty sure I saw it at the Cove earlier today."

You start to feel excited. "That's a great lead. Thanks!"

"Let's head to the Cove," Cadence suggests.

You and Cadence step back into the Plaza when you suddenly freeze.

"Oh no. Raj!" you say, slapping your flipper to your forehead. "I forgot all about him. He's probably wondering where I am."

If you run back to town and get Raj, go to page 63.

If you hurry to the Cove, go to page 79.

CONTINUED FROM PAGE 27.

"Maybe the clue is in Fred the cuckoo clock," you suggest. "Let's check that out."

You and Raj head to the Ski Lodge. When you enter the cozy building, you're surprised to see it crowded with penguins.

"Maybe they're here to look for the clue, too," you guess.

But nobody is paying attention to the cuckoo clock. They're all playing *Find Four*. You head for the clock, but there's no clue.

"Hey, do you want to play?" A penguin is sitting in front of a *Find Four* game. "It's a tournament," he explains.

You and Raj can't resist. You enter the tournament, figuring it won't take up that much time. But you're wrong. You and Raj are on fire! In the end, it's you versus Raj, and you win.

"Woo-hoo!" you cheer. Then you look at the clock. You've missed the secret concert.

"Oh well," you tell Raj. "At least we had fun playing *Find Four*."

THE END

CONTINUED FROM PAGE 47.

You lean to the right—and it turns out you were right! The track curves to the right, and you and Raj maintain your balance.

Your cart swiftly catches up to the one in front of you. The crab is within your reach. You look at Raj.

"Let's do this!" you cry.

You and Raj jump up and land in the cart in front of you! You've done tricks on *Cart Surfer* before, but this beats them all. Your heart is pounding.

You take the clue from the crab's claws. "I'll take that!" you say.

The crab clacks its claws together, annoyed. But you've won. You and Raj steer the cart through the course. When you reach the end of the track at the Mine Shack, the crab jumps out and scurries away. You and Raj jump out of your cart.

"Read the clue," Raj says eagerly.

When things get cold, what you need is heat.
Head to a place that serves a toasty treat.

"It's got to be the Coffee Shop," Raj says.
"They serve a toasty treat that warms you up."

"Or it could be the Pizza Parlor," you point
out. "Pizza is a toasty treat, too."

"So which is it?" Raj asks. "Do you have
another hunch?"

You shake your head. "Not this time," you
admit.

If you look for the next clue in the
Coffee Shop, go to page 23.

If you look for the next clue in the
Pizza Parlor, go to page 75.

CONTINUED FROM PAGE 74.

You and Raj hurry to the Lighthouse. Inside, you find an old barrel of cream soda.

"We just need to roll this down to the site of the avalanche," Raj says. "The movement should shake up the carbonation in the barrel, and the soda will explode and burst through the snow."

You roll the barrel down to the snow mound. Cadence and the white puffle are on top of the hill.

"Here we go!" Raj yells. He pushes the barrel and it rolls into the mound.

Boom! It explodes in a gush of soda, and you can see through to the cave. You and Raj dive in to rescue the puffle, but the explosion causes another avalanche! Before you can get out, more snow falls, trapping you in the cave.

Cadence looks down through the hole. "Don't worry! I'll go get help. Cadence, OUT!"

You're glad help is on the way, but you wish you had been able to rescue the puffles by yourself!

THE END

"Um, Wiz, we're really flattered," you say. "But we only have one day to teach you our routine. I don't think that's enough time."

"Oh, I understand," Wiz says. He's smiling, but he sounds a little bit disappointed. "I'll be in the crowd rooting for you!"

Wiz walks away.

"Boy, he was nice," you say.

Raj nods. "Definitely. Now let's get back to practicing!"

By the time you report to the finals, you've spent hours working on your routine. It's the same one you did at the semifinals, but now it's perfect.

So many penguins have come to see the finals that they can't fit in the Night Club! But you have a special pass Cadence gave you, and you get right in. This time, you'll be dancing up on the stage, right in front of the judges. The other crews are on the stage, nervously waiting for the finals to start.

"Good luck!" you hear someone yell, and you look down and see Wiz at the front of the crowd. He waves. "You rock!"

Cadence takes center stage. "Let's get this party started! It's time to see which crew has what it takes to become my personal dance crew!"

When it's your turn, you and Raj give it your all. It's such a thrill to be dancing onstage! You wonder what it would be like to be on the rooftop with Cadence.

Unfortunately, you'll never know. Cadence announces the winners—it's the pink dance crew! But you and Raj come in second.

"Nice work, you two," she says. "Here's a special prize for you."

She hands you and Raj each a pair of hot sneakers with stripes on them. They're perfect for dancing! You look down and see Wiz is cheering like crazy for you.

You walk to the edge of the stage and give your sneakers to Wiz.

"Thanks, Wiz," you say. "It's great to have a fan like you!"

THE END

CONTINUED FROM PAGE 8.

You decide to trust Raj. How you dance is more important than what you wear, right?

"Let's split up," you say. "I'll see what the other dancers are up to so we can make sure our routine is fresh."

You walk from the Plaza to the Town Center and enter the Night Club. When you get inside, there's a big sign on the wall.

DANCE CREW AUDITIONS CANCELED UNTIL FURTHER NOTICE!
Sorry, Cadence

Then you notice Cadence herself, standing by the stage. She's wearing her usual pink-and-yellow scarf and white sneakers. But she looks upset.

"Cadence, wow, it's cool to meet you in person!" you say. "Is everything okay?"

Cadence shakes her head. "I'm very worried. The green puffle is missing!"

She can only mean one puffle—the green puffle that sits on one of the big speakers inside the Night Club. The happy puffle is always bouncing up and down to the music.

"That's very mysterious," you say.

Cadence nods. "It's been gone for a long time. That's not like it. It's always here!"

You forget all about the canceled dance crew auditions.

"I'll help you look for the puffle," you say.

Cadence perks up. "Really?"

"We need to look for clues," you tell her. "We can start by asking if anyone has seen it."

"Sounds like a plan!" Cadence says.

You approach some penguins on the dance floor. Two are red and two are blue. Each has a flipper on his hip, and is pointing to the ceiling with the other flipper, disco-style.

"Hi," you say. "I'm just wondering. Have you seen the green puffle around lately?"

"No," all four penguins reply at once. They don't stop dancing. "Sorry we can't help."

"No problem," you say.

You and Cadence go around the dance floor, asking about the green puffle. No one has seen it. Then you talk to two penguins with ponytails doing a groovy, sixties-style dance.

"As a matter of fact, I remember seeing it yesterday," one of the penguins says. "It was hopping on the Dance Contest sign-in table. I thought that was a little odd."

"Thanks!" you say. You turn to Cadence. "This could be an important clue."

The sign-in table is right next to the speaker that the green puffle usually bounces on. You head to the table and see a smudge of ink on the sign-in sheet.

"I bet this is where the green puffle landed," you guess.

"Look!" Cadence says, pointing. "There's another smudge on the floor."

You look down and see a small smudge of ink on the gray floor.

"Another clue!" you say. Then you notice another smudge of ink—and it's right in front of a different speaker. This speaker is the secret entrance to the Boiler Room.

"It looks like the green puffle went down to the Boiler Room," you say.

"Wow, you're a really good detective," Cadence says. "Let's check it out."

You and Cadence go inside the speaker and

climb down the ladder into the Boiler Room. You scan the floor for more ink smudges, but you don't see any.

"The ink must have all rubbed off," you guess. "Let's head for the Underground Pool."

You go through the green door and enter the room with the Underground Pool. The swimming penguins are all excited when they see Cadence.

"Can you teach us some dance moves in the water?" one penguin asks.

"Sorry, guys, but I'm here to help solve a mystery," Cadence says. "I'm looking for the green puffle. Have you seen it?"

The penguins all shake their heads. Cadence turns to you.

"Looks like we're out of clues," she says. "What next?"

If you continue on into the Mine Shack, go to page 9.

If you climb up the ladder and go to the Plaza, go to page 54.

"Let's sing 'Rockin' at the Dock,'" you say. "We don't have much time, so we should play it safe."

Kat and Sam pull you aside and quickly teach you the song. It's pretty easy. You just have to spin around a few times and sing, "rock, rock, rock," a lot.

As you're practicing, a red penguin runs up to you.

"You guys are on next," he tells you.

"Don't sweat it, guys," you tell Kat and Sam. "We got this."

The Battle of the Bands emcee announces you to the crowd.

"Get ready to rock with The Migrators!"

Kat taps her stick on her drums. "One, two, three, four!"

Sam starts to sing.

"Rock, rock, rock.

Rockin' at the dock."

You and Raj dance to the music. The crowd seems to like you. After your song ends, it's time to pick a winner. The emcee asks the audience to applaud for their favorite band.

The Migrators get a lot of applause, but a band called the Cart Surfers gets even more.

"We did well, guys," Kat said. "Thanks for helping."

Then you notice four penguins walking toward you. One's yellow, one's blue, one's red, and one's green. They're all wearing cowboy hats and sunglasses.

"Hey, we really like your song," the yellow penguin says. "We're doing a special show tonight. We were wondering if you would open for us."

Suddenly you realize who the penguins are.

"You're Franky!" you exclaim. "You guys are the Penguin Band!"

You can't believe your good luck.

"This is too good to be true," you say. "We wanted to go to the secret show. And now we get to be *in* it!"

THE END

CONTINUED FROM PAGE 78.

"Let's try the Underground Pool," you say. "I have a hunch about it."

You head for the pool the quickest way you know, waddling back to the Plaza. Then you open the manhole and climb down the ladder.

There are a few penguins swimming in the pool. One of them is wearing an inner tube that looks like a duck.

Raj starts looking at the windows. They show a view of the underwater world beneath Club Penguin. Fish peacefully float by. Crabs watch you through the window, clicking their claws.

"I hope the clue's not out there," Raj says.

You walk around the pool, looking down. Then you spot it—a shape on the bottom of the pool. It looks like a bottle of some kind.

"I think I found it!" you cry. Then you dive in. You hold your breath and swim to the bottom. You grab the bottle and swim back to the surface.

Raj is impressed. "Nice job!"

You open the bottle and pull out a folded

46

piece of paper. You are about to open it when a crab suddenly crawls up next to you! The mischievous crustacean plucks the clue from your fingers. Then it scurries away into the Mine.

You jump up, and you and Raj chase after the crab. The crab jumps into a mine cart and ricochets away from you down the track leading deep into the Mine. You and Raj have no choice. You jump into the next cart and follow.

The cart is racing down quickly.

"I haven't played *Cart Surfer* in a while," you tell Raj. "I think there's a curve coming up. Should we lean left or lean right?"

"I don't know!" Raj yells. "But we'd better decide fast!"

If you lean to the left, go to page 16.
If you lean to the right, go to page 35.

CONTINUED FROM PAGE 30.

After seeing everyone's costumes, you think Raj might be on to something.

"Let's go back to the Stage and get those mummy costumes," you say.

The two of you get the mummy costumes and head to the Night Club just in time for the auditions. The place is packed with penguins hoping to become part of Cadence's dance crew.

You notice that the stage with the DJ3K machine is blocked off by red ropes. There is a table set up behind the DJ machine with a sign that reads "Judges." In the first seat is Aunt Arctic, editor of *The Club Penguin Times*. In the second seat is a purple puffle dancing in his chair. And in the third seat is Cadence! As usual, she's wearing her trademark pink-and-yellow scarf, matching wristbands, and white sneakers.

"Hey, everybody, thanks for coming to the audition!" Cadence calls out. "Let's raise the roof on this contest!"

The crowd cheers wildly. "Please line up next to the dance floor," Cadence says. "We'll see one crew at a time."

You're close to the front of the line, so you don't have to wait long for your turn.

"Check it out," Raj says as you walk onto the dance floor. "We're the Funky Mummies!"

A song with a thumping beat begins to play, and you and Raj bust out your best moves.

The music gets faster, and you and Raj move faster. But as you dance and spin, your mummy wraps start to unravel! The wraps get tangled. You and Raj fall on top of each other!

You're so embarrassed. Up at the judge's table, Cadence is smiling.

"Love the cool costumes," she says. "But I need a dance crew who can stay on their toes."

You feel terrible! Cadence must notice the expression on your face.

"Tell you what," she says. "I like your style. Why don't you two help me decorate the rooftop for the concert?"

"Cool!" you and Raj say. Even if you can't be part of Cadence's crew, it will be fun to help with the concert.

THE END

CONTINUED FROM PAGE 24.

"Okay," you say. "We'll try the Ski Hill."

You head to the Ski Village and take the lift up to the top of the hill. Finding the clue is easier than you thought. It's attached to the pole on top of the hill. You jump up and grab it.

"What does it say?" Raj asks.

Finding the final clue will be fun.
Grab a sled and go down Ridge Run.
You'll find the clue if you're at the right speed.
Think carefully about which sled you'll need.

"This sounds pretty easy," Raj says. "We just have to go down the hill."

You walk over to where the sleds are for sale. There's an old-fashioned wood toboggan, and a racing sled that comes in pink or green.

"I'm not sure it's that easy," you say. "Which sled should we choose?"

"The racing sleds go fast," Raj points out. "The clue says we need speed, so we should choose those."

"But the clue says we need the *right*

speed," you tell him. "The right speed could be fast *or* slow. I'm kind of stumped right now."

If you choose the racing sled, go to page 59.

If you choose the toboggan, go to page 71.

CONTINUED FROM PAGE 69.

"Let's stay here," you suggest. "We can watch the dance floor and see what other penguins are doing."

"Sounds good," Raj replies.

Now that the auditions are over, the Night Club is a little less crowded. And as usual penguins from all over are dancing together on the dance floor.

Most of the penguins are waving their flippers and bouncing up and down to the music. But a few are really tearing things up. A couple of penguins are moving their arms like ancient Egyptians. Others are doing the moonwalk.

Then you see an orange penguin break-dancing in the middle of the floor. She's on her back one second spinning and then back on her feet the next.

"Let's try that!" Raj says.

You and Raj practice break-dancing until the next round of auditions. At first, it's not easy. Your spins are out of control. You can't bounce back to your feet quickly enough. But after several tries, you've got it down.

"We will really impress the judges now!" you say.

But what you didn't notice is that some of the other dance crews had the same idea as you. When the round begins, the first crew to go out starts break-dancing!

"What should we do?" you ask Raj.

"It's too late to come up with another routine," Raj points out. "We should stick with our plan and see what happens."

Soon it's your turn. You do your best break dance ever. But when it's time to announce which crews will move on, Cadence has bad news for you.

"Sorry, guys," she says. "You two are great dancers. But we need to see something a little more original."

Then she hands you two T-shirts with a picture of Cadence on them. You and Raj thank her and leave the Night Club.

"At least we came close," you say.

"Yeah," Raj agrees. "Plus, we have these awesome T-shirts to show our friends!"

THE END

CONTINUED FROM PAGES 10, 43.

You and Cadence climb up the ladder in the Underground Pool that leads to the Plaza. A large crowd forms as soon as they spot Cadence.

"Cadence! Is it really you?"

"Cadence, can you teach me some new dance moves?"

Cadence is super nice to her fans, and she takes the time to demonstrate a little spin for the crowd. Soon the Plaza is filled with dancing penguins. You nod to Cadence and the two of you escape into the Pizza Parlor.

Of course, the same thing happens inside the Pizza Parlor. Penguins swarm Cadence, asking for autographs. She happily gives them. The penguins from outside catch on and start flooding the small eatery.

You look around, wondering if you should start asking people about the missing green puffle. Then you see an orange penguin wearing a chef's hat by the beaded curtain that leads into the kitchen. She looks upset.

"What's the matter?" you ask.

"So many customers!" she wails. "I can't

make pizzas fast enough to keep up!"

Cadence overhears. "Sorry about that. I wish I could help, but I've never made a pizza before."

"I'm really good at it," you say. "I always get the maximum score when I play *Pizzatron 3000*."

"Can you help me?" the chef pleads.

You look at Cadence. "I'm not sure what to do. We still have no idea where the green puffle is."

If you leave the Pizza Parlor, go to page 22.

If you stay and help the pizza chef, go to page 31.

"Let's try the Cove first," you suggest.

When you get near the Cove, you're surprised to hear live music in the air. There is a band playing in the sand. Other penguins are standing around listening. Almost everyone is holding an instrument of some kind.

You notice your friends Kat and Sam. Kat is a turquoise penguin with shaggy black hair. She's wearing a puffle T-shirt and holding drumsticks. Sam is a brown penguin with a spiky black hairdo. He's wearing a T-shirt with a recycling symbol on it and has a guitar strapped around his shoulders.

"Hey, guys," you say. "What's going on?"

"It's a Battle of the Bands," Kat explains.

"Cool!" you reply. "You and Sam are in a band, right? Are you going to play?"

Sam frowns. "We wanted to. But our backup singers have colds. We can't go on without them."

"What exactly do they do?" Raj asks.

"They dance along to the music and sing harmonies, mostly," Kat explains.

Raj grins. "Hey, we can do that!"

You like that idea. You know it will put off your chance to find the clue, but it's more fun to help out your friends.

"Just give us a little coaching," you say.

Kat and Sam look at each other and grin. "Awesome!"

You follow them to a quiet spot under the trees to practice.

"We need to pick the right song," Kat says. "We could do 'Rocking at the Dock.' That one has a fast beat."

"Or we could do 'Jet Pack Party,'" Sam suggests. "That always gets the crowd going."

"You're right," Kat says. "But that one's a little more difficult to play."

If you perform "Jet Pack Party," go to page 17.

If you perform "Rockin' at the Dock," go to page 44.

CONTINUED FROM PAGE 24.

You go to the Lighthouse and climb up
the stairs to the Beacon. Raj looks through the
telescope.

"Hey, there's somebody in trouble!" he cries.

A penguin is struggling to stay afloat in
the choppy sea. You and Raj rush down to the
Beach. You throw a life preserver to the penguin
and bring him safely to shore.

"Thank you so much!" he says. "You two are
the best."

"No problem," you say. "We were looking for
a clue to the Penguin Band's secret concert. It's
lucky we spotted you."

"No way!" the penguin says. "I'm the band's
sound engineer. You two can come to the show
as my guests."

You and Raj can't believe your luck. Now
you don't have to look for any more clues!

"Let's go!" you both say at once.

THE END

CONTINUED FROM PAGE 51.

"Come on, let's try the racing sled," Raj urges.

"Okay," you agree. You buy a green racing sled, and you and Raj climb on. Then the two of you speed down the course.

Ridge Run is filled with obstacles and steep bumps. It's all you can do to keep control of the sled.

As you near the end of the run, you see a piece of paper sticking to a tree branch.

"The clue!" you cry.

You reach for it, but the wind from your sled blows it away. You watch helplessly as another wind carries it far, far away.

You feel pretty bad when the sled lands. A penguin holding a stopwatch runs up to you.

"That's the fastest time we've ever recorded on Ridge Run!" he tells you. "You two have set a Club Penguin record!"

You and Raj high-five each other. "Awesome!"

THE END

CONTINUED FROM PAGE 21.

"Um, Wiz, you see, it's like this," you begin.

You look into Wiz's eyes, and he looks so hopeful. You can't bear to let him down.

"We'd love to have you join our crew!" you say.

Wiz jumps up and down. "Oh, thank you, thank you, thank you!" he cries. "I won't let you down!"

"Meet us in my igloo," Raj tells him. "We're gonna need a lot of practice."

"Will do!" Wiz says. "Let me get my dancing shoes!"

You slap your flipper to your forehead. "What are we going to do?" you wonder.

"Everything okay?"

It's Cadence!

"Well, we just added a third member to our dance crew," you tell her.

"Great!" Cadence says. "So why do you look so bummed?"

"Because he can't dance," you tell her.

"*Anyone* can be a good dancer," she says. "You have to help your friend find his groove."

Cadence's advice cheers you up. You head to Raj's igloo for practice. Wiz is already there. At first, you try to teach him your martial arts dance moves. Wiz is a mess. He tries to stand on one foot, but he can't keep his balance at all.

Then you remember Cadence's words.

"So, Wiz," you say. "What do you like to do besides dancing?"

"That's easy," he says. "I love to play *Bean Counters*! It's so much fun to catch those coffee bags as they fly through the air."

Wiz lifts his flippers above his head and waves them back and forth.

"That's it!" you cry. You turn to Raj. "Forget about teaching our moves to Wiz. He can do his *own* moves in time with us."

Raj nods. "It just might work!"

You practice with Raj and Wiz for hours and hours. While you and Raj do your martial arts dance moves, Wiz waves his flippers in the air and runs back and forth, like he's playing *Bean Counters*. It adds a whole new dimension to your dance routine.

On Friday, you perform your routine at the finals, competing against the pink acrobatic dancers and the guys with the fuzzy wigs. Then Cadence announces the winner.

"Raise ya flippers in the air for our winners . . . crew number ten!" she cries. "Their new routine is super solid!"

You're shocked! Then you're swept up in a world of excitement until the concert starts. Cadence takes you to her private dance studio. You plot out the moves for the rooftop show.

Before you know it, it's time for the concert. You head up to the rooftop with Cadence, where the DJ3K machine has been added. A purple penguin with sunglasses is working the machine.

You look down from the rooftop and see a sea of penguins gathered in the Town Center to watch the show. They're clapping and cheering, and the show hasn't even started yet.

"This is awesome!" Raj says.

You nod. "You said it! And we couldn't have done it without Wiz!"

THE END

CONTINUED FROM PAGE 33.

"Who's Raj?" Cadence asks.

"He's my best friend," you say. "He went to the Gift Shop to find costumes for our dance act. We were going to audition for you today."

"Let's go get him," Cadence says. "Then we can all go to the Cove together."

You and Cadence head back to town and find Raj walking around, looking lost.

"There you are!" he cries, running up to you. "I saw that the auditions are canceled. What's going on?"

When Raj sees Cadence behind you, his eyes get wide.

"Whoa, Cadence!" he says. "You are, like, the most awesome dancer."

"Thanks," Cadence says.

You and Cadence tell Raj about your search for the missing green puffle.

"So what are we waiting for?" Raj asks. "Let's get to the Cove!"

When the three of you get to the Cove, it isn't too crowded. A few penguins are checking out the surfboards for sale. You ask them if they've seen the green puffle.

"Nope," a black penguin replies. "But there's a white puffle over by those trees."

He points toward the snow-covered trees behind the Surf Hut.

"Let's check it out," you say. "Maybe the green puffle is there, too."

You walk over to the trees. The white puffle is hiding behind one of the tree trunks, curiously peeking at you.

"What a cute little puffle," Raj says. He reaches into his pocket. "It's a good thing I have some Puffle-Os on me."

Raj holds out the Puffle-Os in his flipper. The little white puffle hops out from behind the tree. It takes a few cautious hops toward Raj. Soon, it's eating right out of his hand.

"Your friend sure has a way with puffles," Cadence says with admiration.

You nod. "Yeah, I guess it's a good thing we brought him along."

"Say there," Raj says to the puffle, "have you seen the green puffle from the Night Club?"

The white puffle starts to hop up and down with excitement.

"I think it knows where the green puffle is!"
Raj cries.

The white puffle starts to quickly hop out
of the Cove. You follow it through the Forest,
through the crowded Plaza, and right to the
Snow Forts.

There's a huge snowball fight going on in
the forts. Snowballs are flying everywhere. It's
hard to see the white puffle with all that snow
flying around.

Suddenly, you realize the white puffle is
gone!

"It must have gotten afraid and left," Raj
reasons.

"We have to find it," you say. "It was leading
us to the green puffle!"

You search all over the Snow Forts, but
there's no sign of it. Then you spot something
strange—a patch of yellow clinging to a green
bush. Raj sees it, too. You and Raj walk over to
the bush and pluck off the patch of yellow.

"Puffle fur," he says. "Yellow puffle fur."

You push the branches of the bush aside
and see a snowy path. You have a suspicion that
this could mean something. But the puffle fur

is yellow, not white, or even green. Should you
follow the path? It could be another dead end.
Or do you head over to the Ice Rink to continue
your search?

**If you move ahead to the Ice Rink,
go to page 11.**

**If you follow the snowy path,
go to page 73.**

CONTINUED FROM PAGE 30.

"Our sweet moves will help us to stand out," you remind Raj. "Besides, it's easy to dance in these outfits. The sneakers have a lot of bounce. Even Cadence wears sneakers."

"Yeah, right!" Raj agrees. "Okay, let's get moving."

You get to the Night Club just a few minutes before the auditions start. The place is crowded with penguins hoping to dance with Cadence at the special rooftop concert.

The stage where the DJ3K machine is located is roped off, and you see three judges sitting at a table there. The first is Aunt Arctic, editor of *The Club Penguin Times*. The second is a purple puffle, which makes sense to you— they're great dancers. And the third is Cadence herself!

She stands up, holding a wireless mic. As usual, she's wearing a pink-and-yellow scarf and matching wristbands.

"Wave ya flippers if you want to audition!" she cries, and everyone cheers. "Please line up next to the dance floor. We'll check out the crews one at a time. The judges and I will choose the ten best crews to move on to the next round of auditions. Let's see ya dance like you've never danced before!"

The dance crew wearing the fairy wings goes first. They look great, but the dancers' wings bump into one another while they do their routine.

"All right, next crew," Cadence says.

You watch the next dance crews. Everyone puts their heart into it, but some are clearly better than others. The best crews have all their moves in sync. They keep perfect time with the music. And they've got great rhythm.

Soon it's your turn. You're nervous at first. But when the music starts, you forget everything except the dance.

You and Raj do the routine you do for fun every day. You flap your flippers up and down. You shimmy from side to side. You move like robots.

When you're done, Cadence smiles at you. "Nice job," she says. "Next!"

You wait on the sidelines while the rest of the crews audition. When everyone has had a turn, Cadence stands up with the mic again.

"Everybody did a great job!" she says. "I wish you could all win. But right now we're going to pick the ten best crews."

Your heart is pounding. Will you make it?

Then Cadence points right at you and Raj!

"Congrats, you two are in," she says. "Your moves were really tight."

"Definitely," Aunt Arctic agrees. "Although I do have some advice for you. If you want to win, you might want to learn some more difficult moves."

Cadence nods. "Right. Step up your game."

You and Raj run outside and both let out a big cheer.

"We need some new moves," you say. "And we only have a few hours before the next round."

"We need some inspiration," Raj says.

If you stay at the Night Club for inspiration, go to page 52.

If you go to the Dojo for inspiration, go to page 18.

CONTINUED FROM PAGE 13.

You and Raj high-five each other.

"We made it!"

Cadence decides to let you hang out with the judges to see which other penguins will be on the crew. You all agree that a crew of pink penguins who do a lot of flips and somersaults is the best addition to the team.

You've got one day to get ready for the concert. You work out a routine with Cadence for the show. You can't believe you're actually being taught by the best dancer on all of Club Penguin! She teaches you a cool new move. You stand sideways, move one foot back, and then hop back with your other foot. Then you raise your flippers and spin. Sweet!

When it's finally time for the show, the Town Center is packed with penguins. The show doesn't disappoint. The crowd goes wild.

As you're dancing, you look at Raj and smile. This is a night you'll never forget!

THE END

CONTINUED FROM PAGE 51.

You decide to use the toboggan. You zip down Ridge Run. On the way down, you snag the clue off of a tree branch.

This place of fire, water, and snow
Is where you'll find the secret show.

"The Dojo!" you and Raj cry together.

The Dojo courtyard is crowded with penguins. You head to the front of the crowd and see the Penguin Band. You've made it!

"Welcome to our secret concert!" the yellow penguin calls out, and you clap and cheer along with everyone else. The drummer counts out a beat, and the band launches into their first song.

You and Raj start tapping your feet. This is awesome! Then a pink penguin comes dancing toward you. It's Cadence!

"Glad to see you two made it," she says.

"Thanks, Cadence!" you reply.

Then you all dance the night away.

THE END

CONTINUED FROM PAGE 76.

"We shouldn't mess with anything new now," you say. "Let's just stick to what we know."

Len, Ben, and Ken push the piano on the stage aside and Len turns on a boom box. As the music blares, Smooth Moves does their routine. They definitely live up to their name.

Then you and Raj go. You're great. But Smooth Moves is better.

Len, Ben, and Ken shake your flippers.

"Nice job," you tell them.

"You too," says Len.

"Guess we'd better go look for that next clue," Raj says with a sigh.

"Don't be silly!" Ken says. "The dance contest was fun. But we don't care about winning. We'll take you to the show with us."

The secret show is at the Dojo. Soon you're dancing in the Dojo courtyard as the Penguin Band plays.

"I'm glad we went to the Pizza Parlor!" Raj says.

THE END

CONTINUED FROM PAGE 66.

Something tells you to follow the snowy path. You decide to listen to your intuition.

"Let's go this way," you say, and Cadence and Raj follow you.

You go a short way when you see the white puffle hopping up and down. You look past it and see a huge mound of snow at the bottom of a hill. The white puffle hops up the mound and you climb up the snow hill after it.

The white puffle stops on the hillside in front of a small hole. You look through and gasp.

A green puffle and yellow puffle are down there! They seem to be in some kind of a cave, and you realize the cave is blocked by the mound of snow.

"They're trapped!" you cry.

Cadence looks down into the cave. "Are you okay? What happened?"

Luckily, the yellow puffle is a good actor. Through its pantomime, you realize it was playing the flute while the green puffle danced. The vibrations caused an avalanche. They hid in the cave, but now they're trapped.

"We've got to rescue them!" Cadence cries.

You have spent some time rescuing puffles before, playing *Puffle Roundup*. You try to think of the best thing to do.

"We could find a rope," you suggest. "Then we could lower it through the hole and try to lift the puffles out of there."

"That could be dangerous," Raj says. "The puffles might swing back and forth on the rope and hurt themselves. I say we find some way to blast through the snow."

If you use a rope to rescue the penguins, go to page 25.

If you blast through the snow, go to page 37.

CONTINUED FROM PAGE 36.

"Let's try the Pizza Parlor first," you say.

When you get to the Pizza Parlor, you see three familiar penguins sitting at a table. They're a dance crew you've seen practicing at the Night Club. Their names are Len, Ken, and Ben, but they call themselves Smooth Moves.

The three penguins are light blue and are all wearing white suits.

"Hey there!" Len calls out to you.

You and Raj walk over to their table.

"What's up, guys?" Ken asks.

You hold up the invitation Cadence gave you. "We have an invitation to the secret show today. We're looking for the next clue."

"Cool," Ben says. "We have an invitation, too. But we found all our clues already. We're just hanging out until the show starts."

Raj's eyes light up. "Can you tell us where it is?"

The three penguins lean in and whisper to one another. Then Len speaks up.

"Let's make it fun," he says. "We challenge you to a dance contest, right here, right now.

We'll let the crowd here decide. If you two win, we'll tell you the location."

You and Raj look at each other and nod. That *does* sound like fun.

"We're in!"

You and Raj go to a quiet corner to discuss your routine.

"We should do what we practiced, right?" you ask.

"I think we should try the Hip-Hop Hurricane," Raj says.

You gasp. "That move is so hard! We never get it right."

Raj nods toward Smooth Moves. "Those guys are the best. We'll never win if we don't try something big."

If you decide to try the Hip-Hop Hurricane, go to page 14.

If you and Raj stick with your old routine, go to page 72.

CONTINUED FROM PAGE 27.

"Let's check out the Clock Tower," you suggest. "It's the biggest clock on the island."

You go back down the snowy path to the Snow Forts to examine the clock. You walk around it, trying to find some kind of clue.

Raj spots one. "There's something sticking out of that gear."

The clock is powered by snowballs. Penguins throw snowballs at a round target sticking out of the side of the large clock. The target is attached by rods to several gears that turn when the target is hit.

You look up and see a folded piece of paper sticking out of one of the big, metal gears that powers the clock. It's too high to climb up and get it—but you know you don't have to.

"We just need to throw snowballs at the target," you say. "The gears will turn, and the clue will fall to the ground."

At least, you hope that will happen. You and Raj quickly start making snowballs. You start hurling them at the target.

"Bull's-eye!" Raj shouts as your snowballs

hit their mark. The gears turn, and just as you predicted, the piece of paper flutters to the snowy ground. You rush to grab it.

"What does it say?" Raj asks eagerly.

You read the clue aloud:

Water, water, everywhere.
That's got to make you think.
The next clue's in a watery spot.
But it's not water you would drink.

"Hmm," you say thoughtfully. "The clue might be at the Underground Pool. You can swim in that water, but you can't drink it."

"Maybe it's the water at the Cove," Raj suggests. "You can swim there, too. But that's salt water. You can't drink that, either."

If you look for the next clue in the Underground Pool, go to page 46.

If you look for the next clue in the Cove, go to page 56.

CONTINUED FROM PAGE 33.

"Let's hurry to the Cove," you say. "It's a good lead. And Raj is a good friend—he'll understand."

You and Cadence hurry to the Cove. You notice a wild white puffle hopping around under the snowy trees.

"Maybe that puffle has seen the green puffle," you say. But when you approach the white puffle, it runs away.

I should have brought Raj with me, you realize. *He's great with puffles!*

Next, you and Cadence talk to the penguins there, but no one has seen the green puffle. You suddenly have an idea.

"Why don't I do a search from above?" you suggest. "I can play *Jet Pack Adventure* and look for the green puffle from the air."

"Sounds good," Cadence agrees. "I'll keep looking on the ground. We can meet back at the Night Club."

You quickly head to the Beacon to play *Jet Pack Adventure*. You begin to fly in a circular pattern around the island. You're so busy looking for the green puffle that you don't notice that your fuel tank is empty!

You begin to plummet toward the ground. You activate your parachute, but it won't open. The ground is speeding toward you. You close your eyes . . .

Suddenly, you feel light, like you are floating. You open your eyes and see a giant bubble around you. The bubble gently lowers you to the ground.

Confused, you see a purple puffle with a bubble blower nearby. The puffle has saved you! You want to thank it, but it quickly hops away.

You head back to the Night Club. Cadence is outside—and she's holding the green puffle!

"A bunch of puffles brought it to me," she tells you. "I think they saved it from some kind of danger."

"A puffle saved me, too," you say, telling her the story. "How strange! I went out to save a puffle and a puffle saved me, instead!"

THE END